WHAT'S UNDER THE BED?

For Mum & Iji

To all my nieces and nephews who have been a constant inspiration throughout the making of this book.

SIMON & SCHUSTER BOOKS FOR YOUNG READERS
An imprint of Simon & Schuster Children's Publishing Division
1230 Avenue of the Americas, New York, New York 10020
Copyright © 2008 by Joe Fenton
All rights reserved, including the right of reproduction in whole or in part in any form.
SIMON & SCHUSTER BOOKS FOR YOUNG READERS is a trademark of Simon & Schuster, Inc.
Book design by Lucy Ruth Cummins · The text for this book is set in Century Schoolbook.
The illustrations for this book are rendered in mixed media.
Manufactured in China
2 4 6 8 10 9 7 5 3 1
Library of Congress Cataloging-in-Publication Data
Fenton, Joe.
What's under the bed? / written and illustrated by Joe Fenton—1st ed.
p. cm.
Summary: When Fred lays down his head, he imagines there is something
monstrous under his bed.
ISBN-13: 978-1-4169-4943-5 (alk. paper)
ISBN-10: 1-4169-4943-7 (alk. paper)
[1. Bedtime—Fiction. 2. Fear of the dark—Fiction.
3. Imagination—Fiction. 4. Stories in rhyme.] I. Title. II. Title: What
is under the bed?
PZ8.3.O988Whc 2008
[E]—dc22
2007032558

WHAT'S UNDER THE BED?

Written and illustrated by Joe Fenton

Simon & Schuster Books for Young Readers
New York   London   Toronto   Sydney

"Time for bed, Fred!"

What's that sound?

Is there
something on
the ground?

Could there be something under my bed?

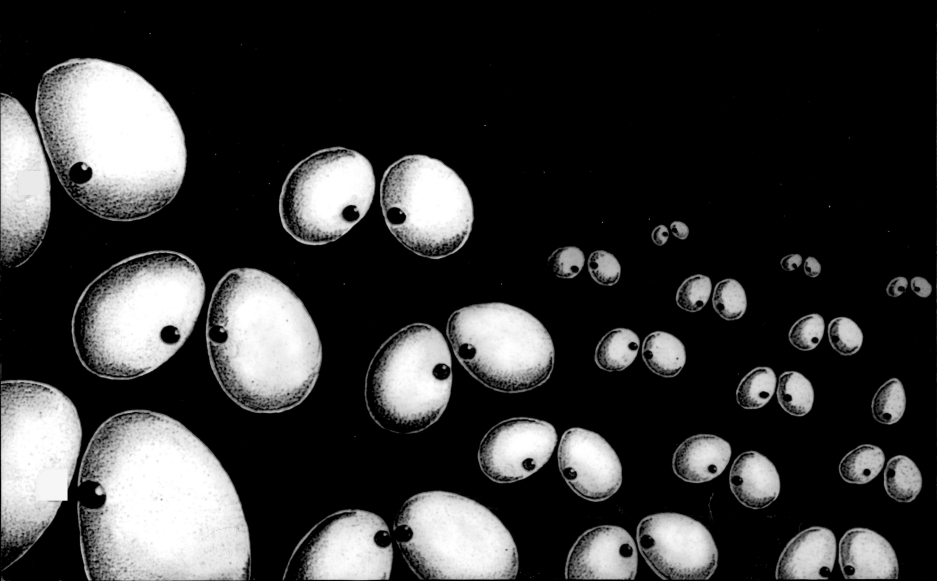

Could it be green?

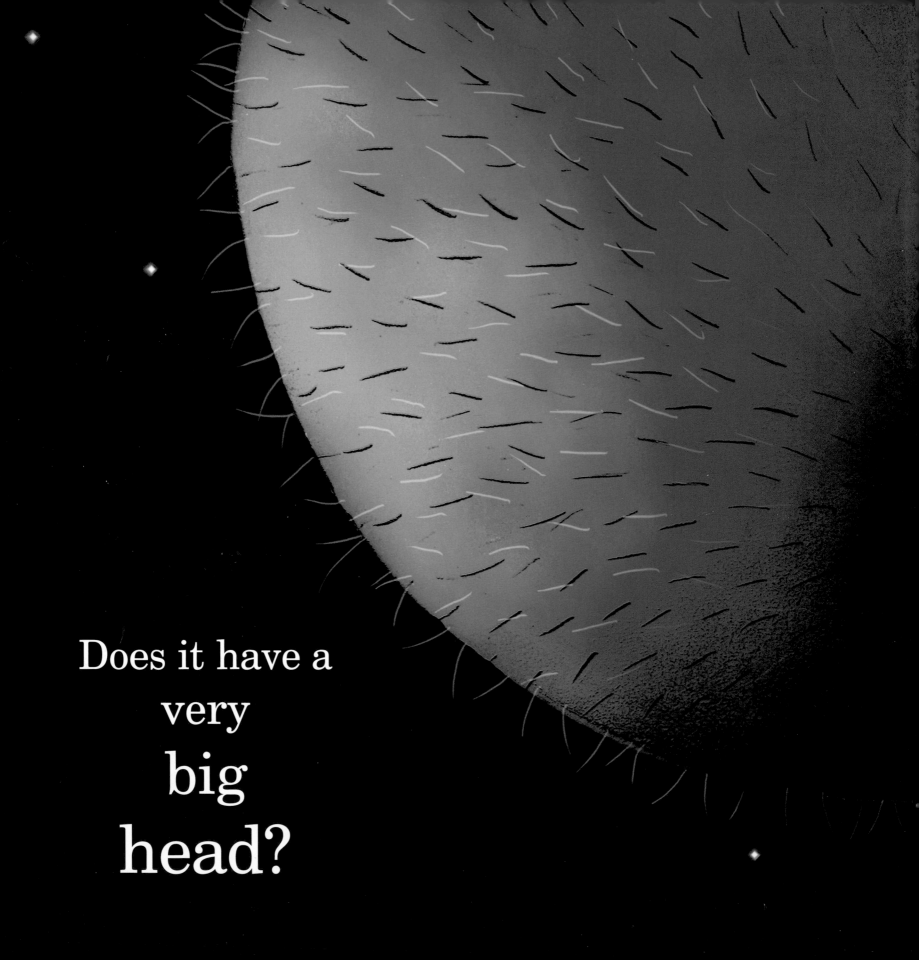

Does it have a
very
big
head?

Is it tall?

Or rather small?

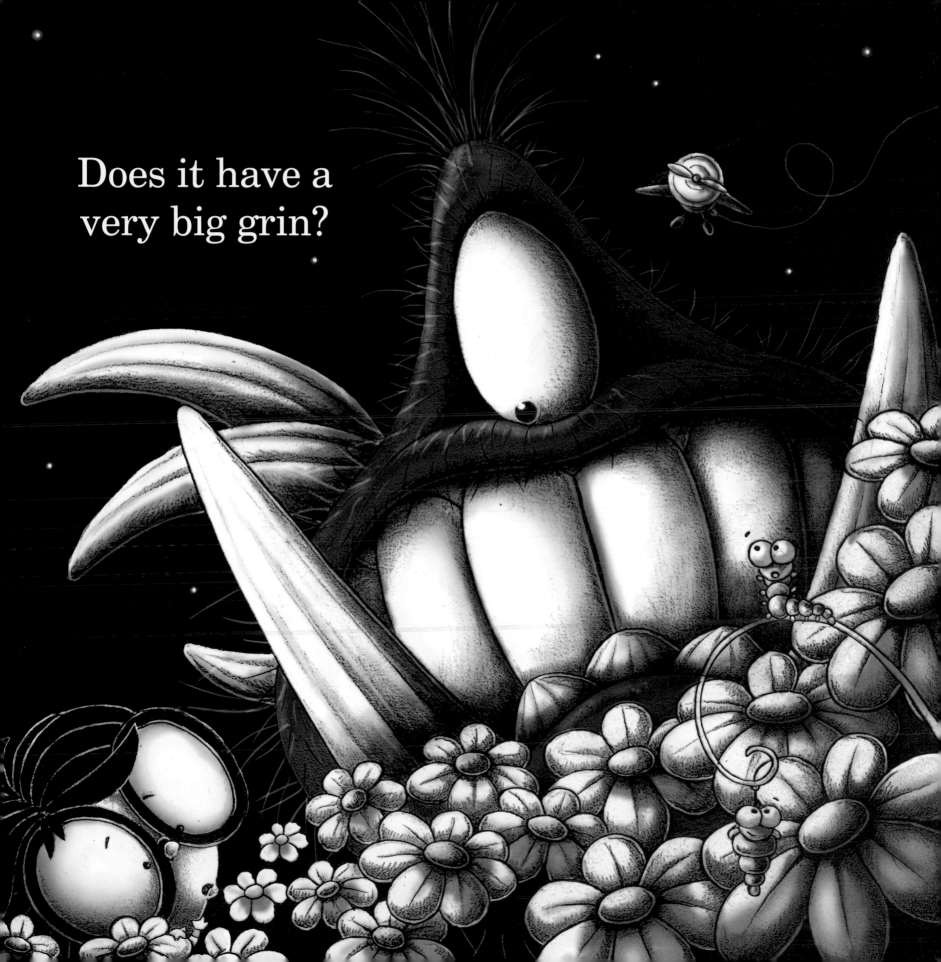

Does it have a
very big grin?

Does it have
long nails?

Oh, I hope it's been fed!

Or it might eat my bed!

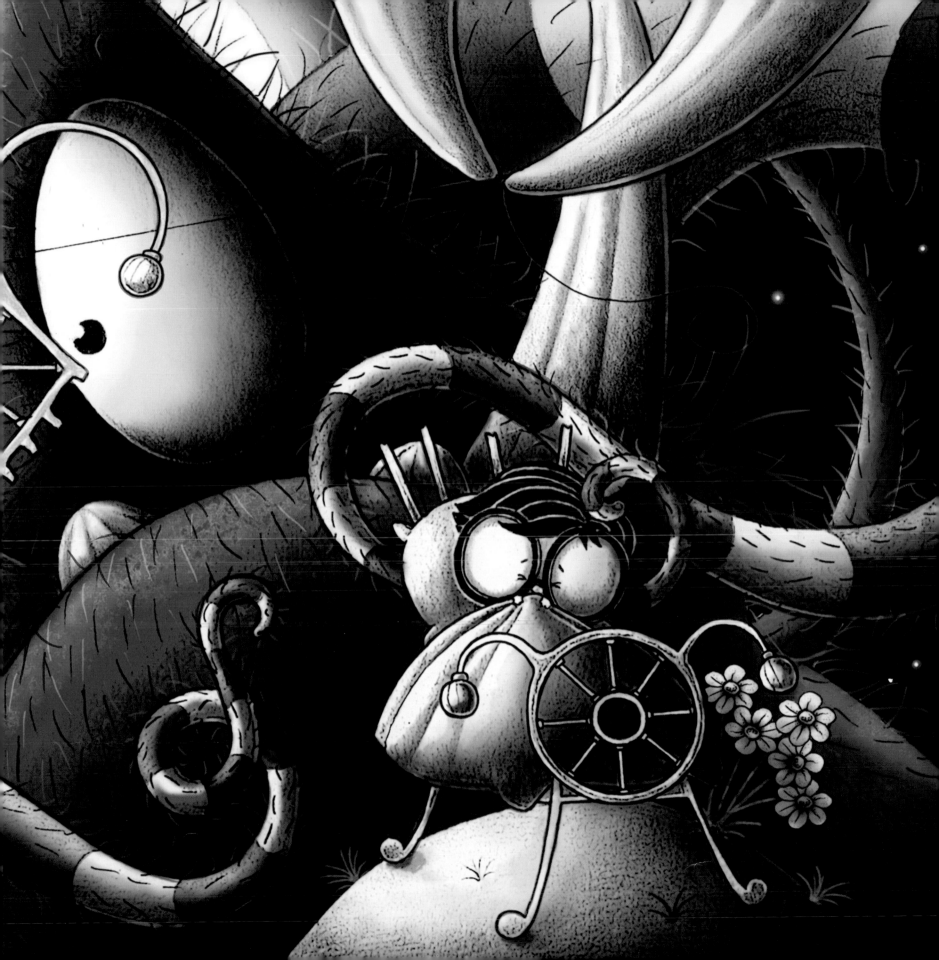

Okay, one, two, three, four . . .

It's time to look
on the floor!

Hey, it's only Ted!

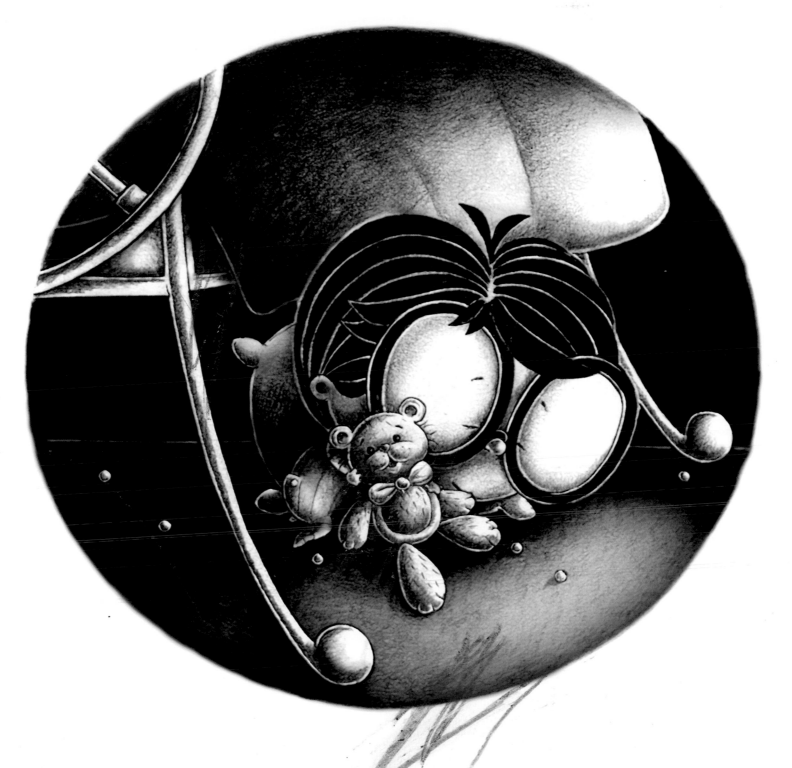

There's nothing scary here under the bed.

What's that noise? What's that sound?
Is there something on the ground?